The Rich Man
and the Shoe-maker

The Rich Man

A FABLE BY LA FONTAINE

and the Shoe-maker

ILLUSTRATED BY BRIAN WILDSMITH

OXFORD
UNIVERSITY PRESS

Once upon a time there lived
a poor but cheerful shoe-maker.

He was so happy he sang all day long.
The children loved to stand round his
window to listen to him.

Next door to the shoe-maker lived a rich man.

He used to sit up all night to count his gold.

In the morning he went to bed, but he could not sleep because of the sound of the shoe-maker's singing.

One day he thought of a way of stopping the singing.

He wrote a letter to the shoe-maker asking him to call.

The shoe-maker came at once, and to his surprise the rich man gave him a bag of gold.

When he got home again, the shoe-
maker opened the bag. He had never
seen so much money before! He sat
down at his bench and began, carefully,
to count it. The children watched
through the window.

There was so much there
that the shoe-maker was
afraid to let it out of his
sight. So he took it to bed
with him.

But he could not sleep for worrying
about it. So he got out of bed and

went to hide it in the attic, but he was not sure if that was a good place.

Very early in the morning he got up and brought his gold down from the attic. He had decided to hide it up the chimney instead.

But after breakfast he thought it
would be safer in the chicken-house.
So he hid it there.

But he was still uneasy and in a little while he dug
a hole in the garden, and buried his bag of gold in it.

It was no use trying to work. He was too worried about the safety of his gold. And as for singing, he was too miserable to utter a note. He could not sleep, or work, or sing — and, worst of all, the children no longer came to see him.

At last the shoe-maker felt so unhappy that he seized his bag of gold and ran next door to the rich man. 'Please take back your gold,' he said. 'The worry of it is making me ill and I have lost all my friends. I would rather be a poor shoemaker, as I was before.'

And so the shoe-maker was
happy again, and sang all day
at his work.

OXFORD
UNIVERSITY PRESS

Great Clarendon Street, Oxford OX2 6DP

Oxford University Press is a department of the University of Oxford.
It furthers the University's objective of excellence in research, scholarship,
and education by publishing worldwide in

Oxford New York

Athens Auckland Bangkok Bogotá Buenos Aires Calcutta
Cape Town Chennai Dar es Salaam Delhi Florence Hong Kong Istanbul
Karachi Kuala Lumpur Madrid Melbourne Mexico City Mumbai
Nairobi Paris São Paulo Singapore Taipei Tokyo Toronto Warsaw

with associated companies in Berlin Ibadan

Oxford is a registered trade mark of Oxford University Press
in the UK and in certain other countries

First published 1965
Reprinted 1966, 1968, 1970, 1972, 1979, 1986, 1990, 1992
First published in paperback 1983
Reprinted 1985, 1990, 1991
Reissued in paperback 1999

ISBN 0-19-272402-9

Printed in Hong Kong